My First NFL Book

LOS ANGELES RAMS

Nate Cohn

LET'S READ
AV²
BY WEIGL™
ADDED VALUE • AUDIO VISUAL

Go to **www.av2books.com**, and enter this book's unique code.

BOOK CODE

P 9 6 5 2 4 2

AV² by Weigl brings you media enhanced books that support active learning.

7356623

AV² provides enriched content that supplements and complements this book. Weigl's AV² books strive to create inspired learning and engage young minds in a total learning experience.

Your AV² Media Enhanced books come alive with...

Audio
Listen to sections of the book read aloud.

Video
Watch informative video clips.

Embedded Weblinks
Gain additional information for research.

Try This!
Complete activities and hands-on experiments.

Key Words
Study vocabulary, and complete a matching word activity.

Quizzes
Test your knowledge.

Slide Show
View images and captions, and prepare a presentation.

... and much, much more!

Published by AV² by Weigl
350 5th Avenue, 59th Floor
New York, NY 10118

Website: www.av2books.com

Library of Congress Control Number: 2017930546

ISBN 978-1-4896-5556-1 (hardcover)
ISBN 978-1-4896-5558-5 (multi-user eBook)

Printed in the United States of America in Brainerd, Minnesota
1 2 3 4 5 6 7 8 9 0 21 20 19 18 17

032017
020317

Editor: Katie Gillespie
Art Director: Terry Paulhus

Weigl acknowledges Getty Images and iStock as the primary image suppliers for this title.

My First NFL Book

LOS ANGELES RAMS

CONTENTS

2 AV² Book Code

4 Team History

6 The Stadium

8 Team Spirit

10 The Jerseys

12 The Helmet

14 The Coach

16 Player Positions

18 Star Player

19 Famous Player

20 Team Records

22 By the Numbers

24 Quiz/Log on to www.av2books.com

Team History

The Los Angeles Rams joined the NFL in 1937. They started playing football in Ohio. The team moved to California and played for Los Angeles from 1946 to 1994. The Rams then went to St. Louis, Missouri. The team moved back to Los Angeles in 2016.

Georgia Frontiere was the Rams' owner from 1979 to 2008. She is in the team's Ring of Honor.

The Stadium

The Rams play at Los Angeles Memorial Coliseum. The stadium opened in 1923. It is a landmark. This means that many people know about it. The Rams will play at Los Angeles Stadium at Hollywood Park once it is built.

Two Summer Olympic Games have been held at the Coliseum in Los Angeles, California.

Team Spirit

Rampage is the Rams' mascot. He leads cheers while running on the sidelines. The word "rampage" means "to run wild." This is why his name suits him. Rampage seems to run everywhere he goes.

Rampage visits schools to root for kids and help them stay active.

The Jerseys

The Rams started wearing blue and yellow in 1938. The yellow changed to gold in 2000. The Rams are one of the few teams that usually wear white shirts at home games. Most teams wear their more colorful jerseys at home.

The Helmet

The Rams' helmets do not show the team logo. They have curls of color that look like ram horns instead. The Rams have worn horns on their helmets in a number of colors. The curls have been white, yellow, and even shiny gold.

The Rams were the first team in the NFL to decorate their helmets.

The Coach

Sean McVay became the Rams' head coach at the end of the 2016 season. He is the youngest head coach in NFL history. He was 30 years old when the Rams hired him. McVay coached the offense of several NFL teams before joining the Rams. He is the Rams' 23rd head coach.

Player Positions

Each team has backup players. They are called the second string. These players may enter the game if other players get hurt. Backups may also be called to the field in place of players who get too tired. Some players are on the second string for more than one position.

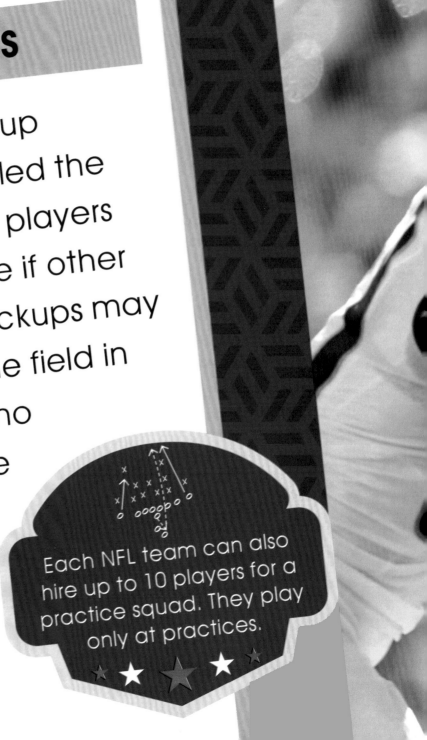

Each NFL team can also hire up to 10 players for a practice squad. They play only at practices.

16

Todd Gurley was drafted by the Rams in 2015. He was an NFL Rookie of the Year. A rookie is a person in his first season. He also played in the Pro Bowl his first year. That is a special game for the NFL's best players. This running back gains yards through strength as much as speed. Gurley is hard to tackle.

Marshall Faulk was a running back when the Rams won the Super Bowl for the 1999 season. He was part of the "Greatest Show on Turf." That is what reporters called the Rams' offense. The word "turf" is another name for the field. Faulk was the second player in NFL history to both rush and receive more than 1,000 yards in the same season.

Team Records

The Rams have won three NFL championships. Mike Martz was the coach of the Rams' offense in 1999. His offensive team scored 526 points that season. They won the Super Bowl that year. Quarterback Kurt Warner won the first of his two Most Valuable Player awards that same season.

3 NFL Championships

Mike Martz

1999 Offense Scored 526 Points

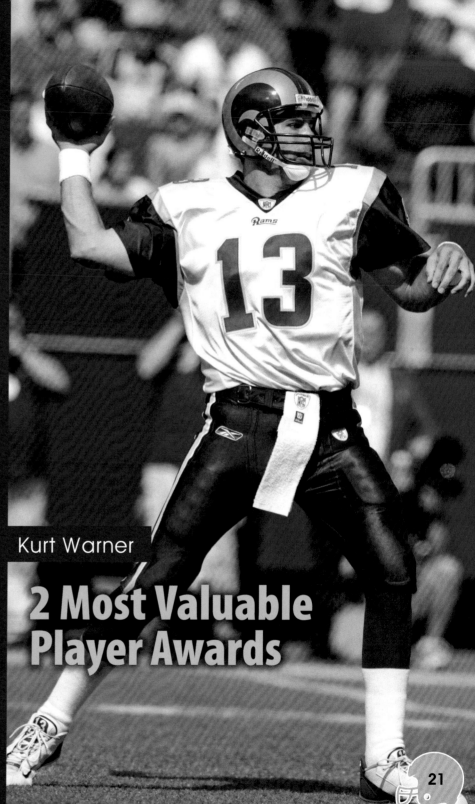

Kurt Warner

2 Most Valuable Player Awards

21

By the Numbers

Kicker Jeff Wilkins scored **1,223 points** as a Rams player.

The Rams had **9** wins in 1945. This was their **first** winning season.

The Rams' new stadium will cost **$2.6 billion.**

Kurt Warner has a Super Bowl record for throwing **414 yards.**

The Rams were the **first** NFL team to score at least **500 points** for **3 seasons** in a row.

Running back Eric Dickerson set a **2,105-yard** NFL single-season rushing record in 1984.

Quiz

1. In which state did the Rams first play?

2. In what year did the Rams move to Los Angeles for the second time?

3. Who is the youngest head coach in NFL history?

4. Who was the running back in the "Greatest Show on Turf"?

5. How many Most Valuable Player awards did Kurt Warner win?